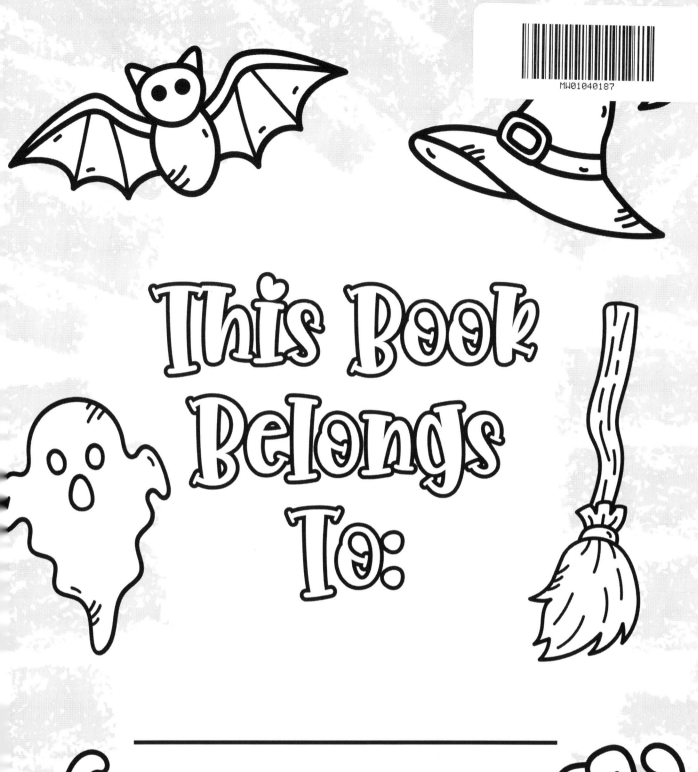

This Book Belongs To:

_____

MIGHTY SPROUTS
PUBLISHING

Pumpkin

Witch

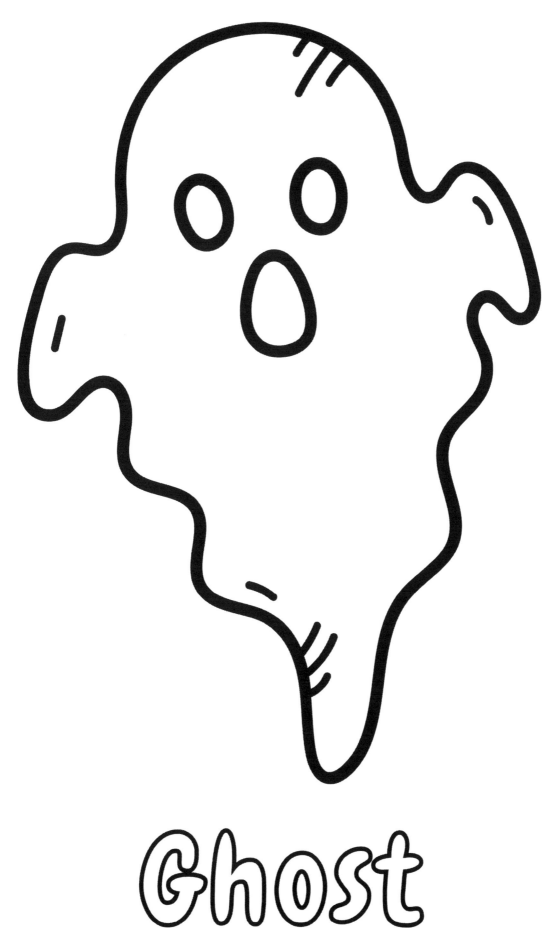

Ghost

Hat

Broom

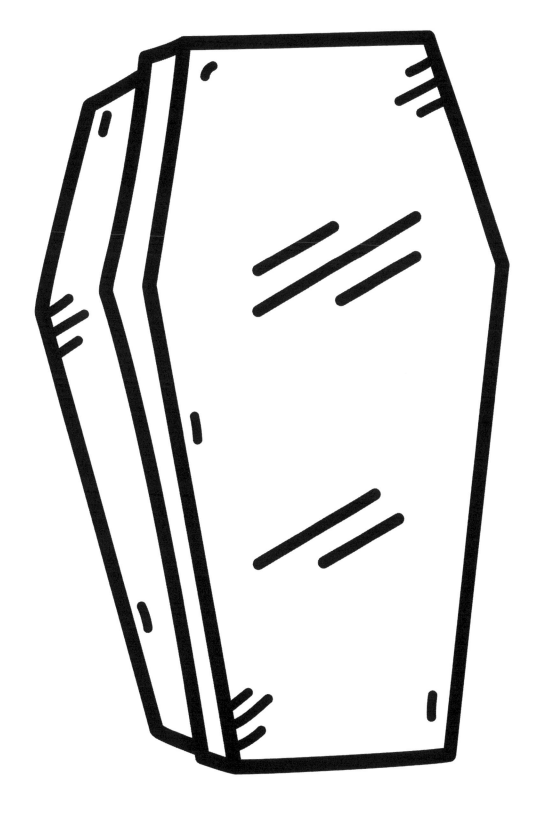

Casket

Skull

Candle

Bottle

Hand

Frankenstein

Headstone

Candy

Cauldron

Reeper

Doll

Bats

Warewolf

Cat

Pumpkins

Candy Bucket

Mummy

Spider

Vampire

Eyeballs

Cat

Scarecrow

A Scare

Candy Corn

Skull Globe

Leaves

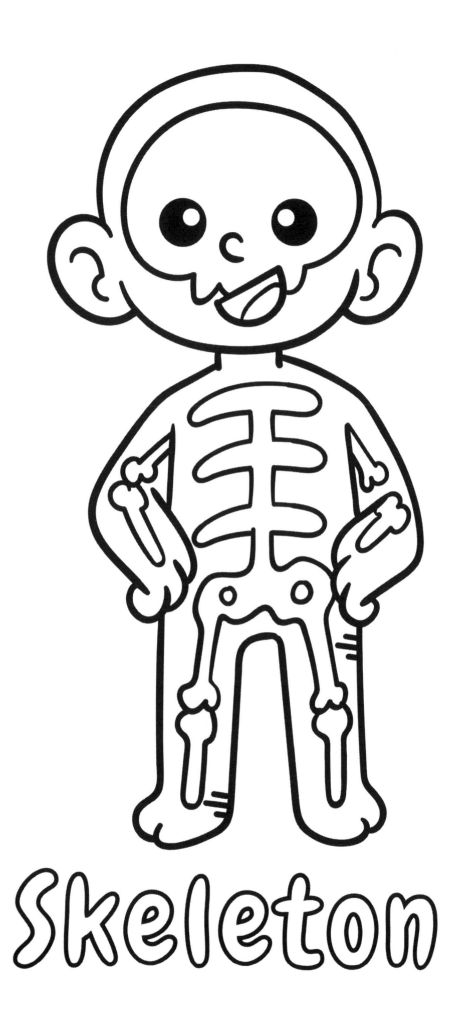

Skeleton

Haunted House

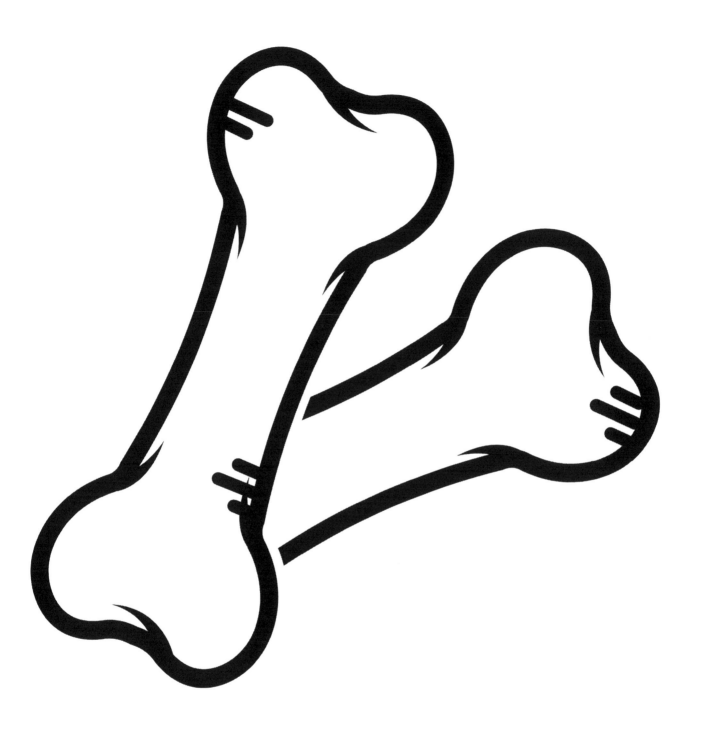

Bones

Cupcake

Bob For Apples

Ice Cream

Monster

Zombie

Pumpkin

Caramel Apple

Balloons

Potions

Moon

Lolipop

Book

Calendar

Ghosts

Tree

Spider Web